A DAY AT THE CIRCUS

CARL AND CINDY SERIES

To my wonderful children
Isabel, Nicole,
Kimberly and Justin.

Published by Jink Publishing

Unit 33699, PO Box 6945, London, W1A 6US United Kingdom

ISBN: 978-1-914235-01-6

Copyright @ Jink Publishing 2020
First Printed 2020

Books in this series:

Dad looked up from his newspaper one evening. "The circus is in town," he said. "Who wants to go to the circus?"

1

"Me!" shouted Cindy. "Yes, please!" said Carl. "When?" "We can go tomorrow night," said Dad. "You three go," said Mom, "I'll stay home and look after Roxy."

2

The next day Cindy and Carl were very excited! Nothing they did seemed to make the day go faster. It seemed to drag on forever!

3

Dad, Cindy, and Carl said goodbye to Roxy and Mom, then climbed into the car. Dad parked their car in a big field next to a huge tent.

4

"There are so many cars!" marveled Cindy. "That's because lots of people are going to see the circus tonight," said Dad.

5

Dad held onto Cindy's and Carl's hands so that they didn't get lost in the crowd. There were many people lining up to get into the tent!

When they were finally inside the tent, the open area in the middle was lit up with bright lights. They shuffled forward and found their seats near the front. "Wow, Dad," said Carl. "This is amazing!"

Once everyone had sat down, the circus began. Loud music played while six beautiful women on white horses galloped into the arena. "Wow," whispered Cindy, "they're so pretty!"

The women did amazing tricks on the backs of their horses, turning their bodies upside down and balancing on just one hand. "Ooooh!" breathed Cindy.

Next a man in a suit and a big hat came in with a long whip. 'Why does he have a whip?' whispered Carl. "Shhh!
Wait and see," whispered Dad.

10

Into the arena ran three large lions. Cindy screamed. "They'll eat him!" she said, raising her feet off the floor, anxiously. The man cracked his whip on the floor. It made a loud noise.

All three lions lay down. He cracked it again and they obediently rolled onto their backs. "They're tame," whispered Dad. "He's a lion-tamer."

A man with a white painted face and a red nose suddenly ran into the arena. He got a huge fright when he saw the lions lying there and his pants fell down. He ran out again quickly. "That's a clown," explained Carl. "I know!" said Cindy.

After all three lions had jumped through a hoop, they left the arena. Now the clowns had their turn. They played many funny pranks on each other and made Dad, Cindy, and Carl laugh!

14

They had been so busy watching the clowns that they hadn't noticed the tightrope-walker climb up the ladder. He stepped out onto the thin rope high above their heads. Cindy gasped!

15

The clowns were also worried the tight rope-walker would fall. They ran around on the ground, looking up at him and bumping into each other! Luckily, he didn't fall.

16

After the tightrope-walker walked all the way across, he began walking back again. But in the middle, he stopped, sat down on the thin rope, and then lay down on it. "He's really good," said Dad, admiringly.

Next came the trapeze artists. They swung back and forth on big swings that were attached to the roof of the tent, high above the people.

18

Suddenly, a girl trapeze artist did a somersault in the air, only for her hands to be caught by a man hanging on by his knees!

Cindy could not believe it! Every time the girl let go of one man's hands to somersault through the air, Cindy held her breath and closed her eyes. What if the girl fell? Luckily, she never fell.

20

At the end of the night, the white horses came out again, only this time the women riding them were dressed in sparkly gold.

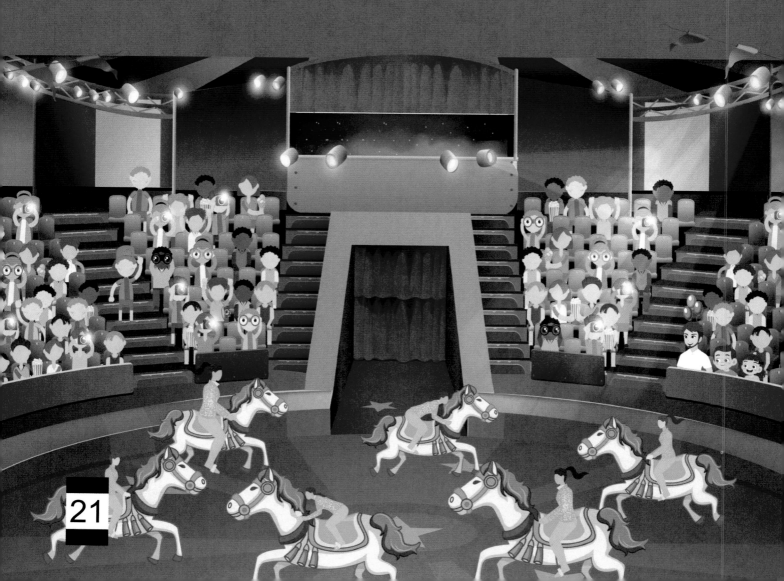

They stood up on the backs of their horses, waving to the audience. Cindy waved back.

Back in the car, Cindy and Carl couldn't stop talking about what they'd seen at the circus that night. When they got home, they told Mom all about it.

"When I grow up, I might want to join the circus," said Cindy. "I'd like to ride a white horse."

Made in the USA
Middletown, DE
11 October 2022

12499422R00015